Dear Saylor—

I am so glad that you ~~~~~~~ by the Seashore. It is a wonderful place to live. I hope you have many fun adventures playing in the sand and the ocean in San Diego.

Love, Nana Lama

November

Saylor
ON THE Seashore

Tonya Calvert

Illustrated by Alejandro Echavez

Saylor on the Seashore

Summary: Inspired by true events. Saylor is a young seagull who is often motivated by his tummy rather than his wits, but living on the Florida Panhandle is dangerous. With fishermen everywhere, a little seagull must rely on what he has been taught to survive. That is, until lunchtime, when Saylor forgets all the warnings his friends have given him. When he finds himself in serious trouble, his friends set out to help. Come to the seashore and cheer them on.

Clear Fork Publishing
P.O. Box 870
102 S. Swenson
Stamford, Texas 79553
(325)773-5550
www.clearforkpublishing.com

Printed and Bound in the United States of America.

ISBN - 978-1-946101-20-4
LCN - 2017940070

Clear Fork Publishing

To Joshua, Nathan, and Joseph for teaching me to see the world through the eyes of a child.
To Jonathan for believing in me. - Tonya

To my wife, Janet, for her ongoing support and my daughters, Michelle and Kaylee. - Alejandro

Saylor was a young seagull who lived with Momma and Poppa Seagull on the seashore down in the Panhandle, deep in the South.

Momma and Poppa Seagull taught Saylor how to hunt for minnows, worms, and crabs to eat.

Momma and Poppa Seagull
also taught Saylor to stay away from
the fishermen with long poles, shiny
hooks, and big nets.

Down by the pier, Old Gray Pelican waited for Saylor to visit. Every day Saylor listened to the wise advice and stories of Old Gray Pelican by the pier, on the shore down in the Panhandle, deep in the South.

Old Gray Pelican told Saylor the story of his friend Big Blue Heron. Big Blue wears a hook in his beak. A fisherman's hook caught him one day long ago, and it's been there ever since.

Old Gray Pelican
warned Saylor not to go near
the fishermen on the shore
down in the Panhandle, deep
in the South.

Old Gray Pelican told Saylor the
story of his friend, Señor Mackerel, the
Spanish Mackerel.

Señor Mackerel was caught in a fishing net. He had been swimming too close
to the shore.

Old Gray Pelican warned
Saylor to stay away from the
fishermen on the shore down in
the Panhandle, deep in the South.

Old Gray Pelican told Saylor the story of his friend, Piper the little Sandpiper, who was caught in a fishing line. She had been looking for supper too close to the fishermen when she was caught.

Old Gray Pelican warned Saylor to stay away from the fishermen on the shore down in the Panhandle, deep in the South.

Saylor thanked Old Gray
Pelican for his stories and promised
to stay away from the fishermen.

But Saylor was hungry... very hungry...

He was thinking about lunch
— minnows, worms, and crabs.
He was not thinking about the
fishermen with long poles, shiny
hooks, and big nets.

The fishermen were looking for their lunch too, with their long poles, shiny hooks, and big nets.

Suddenly Saylor felt something around his leg. It tight-
ened around him, and he could not fly. Saylor was frightened.
He cried loudly.

Momma and Poppa Seagull heard Saylor's cries, and they came.

They brought the whole flock
with them. They all flew around the
fishermen, but none of them knew how
to help Saylor.

Old Gray Pelican heard the cries and knew just what to do. He called on his friends to help Saylor.

First came Big Blue Heron. He pecked at the fishing line that was tangled around Saylor.

Next came Señor Mackerel. He nipped at the fisherman's toes to distract him.

Last came Piper the Sandpiper. She brought encouragement to Saylor. Piper chirped, "Your friends are all here, Saylor! Don't be afraid. We will help you."

Saylor felt the fishing line begin to loosen. Soon, it fell away. He was free! Everyone cheered.

Saylor still visits Old Gray Pelican every day, but now he listens more closely and always avoids the fishermen in the shallow water near the shore down in the Panhandle, deep in the South.

Tonya Calvert
Author

Tonya Calvert enjoys writing children's stories, short stories and creating watercolor art. She finds inspiration all around her, especially on nature walks and at her favorite destination, the Florida Gulf Coast. She has a BS from Columbus State University and a JD from Atlanta's John Marshall Law School. She paused her legal career to homeschool her children and has never looked back. She's been married to her high school sweetheart for 24 years. They live a blessed life in the Deep South with their 3 boys.

http://www.tonyacalvert.com

Alejandro Echavez
Illustrator

Alejandro Echavez is a Freelance Illustrator, Painter and Animator specializing in children's illustrations. He currently resides in Long Island NY, but spent his formative years in Bogota, Colombia, where he first showed an interest in art at the very young age of 6. More than an interest, it was a natural talent that his family nurtured and developed. A kid at heart, his artwork is often colorful and playful in theme. He is not scared of bright colors, which he uses to create movement and vibrancy in his work. Alejandro is currently working on children's books and continues creating the vivid canvases and artwork he is known for.

www.alejoartworks.com

CPSIA information can be obtained
at www.ICGtesting.com
Printed in the USA
BVHW020634180719
553786BV00012B/101/P